Rumpelstiltskin

Written by Abie Longstaff
Illustrated by Caroline Romanet

Collins

Once upon a time there lived a girl who was poor but clever. Her name was Daisy, for she was as fair as a flower.

Every day she watched the handsome king riding by.
"He's so brave!" she thought.

One day, Daisy announced, "I want to marry the king!"
Everyone laughed.
"A poor girl can't marry a king!"

Daisy's father was not as clever as his daughter, but he wanted to make her happy.
He went to see the king. "My daughter can spin straw into gold," he boasted.

So the king called for Daisy, and took her to a room full of straw.

"Spin this straw into gold by morning," he said, locking the door.

Daisy sat and wept. She did not know how to spin straw into gold! She was so embarrassed. The king would never marry her now!

"Everyone will laugh at me again," she sobbed. "Oh help!"

Suddenly a trap door opened in the floor and out jumped a goblin.
"I will help you," he promised, "if you give me your necklace."
Daisy agreed and, to her amazement, the goblin spun the straw into gold.

In the morning, the king was happy.
But seeing the gold made him greedy.
He took Daisy to a bigger room filled with straw.
"I want more gold by morning," he demanded.

Again Daisy called for help.
Again the goblin came.
"I will help you," he promised,
"if you give me your ring."
Daisy agreed, and the goblin spun the straw into gold.

Now the King was very happy, but he wanted still more gold.

He took Daisy to the biggest room in the palace, which was filled with straw.

"If you can spin all of this straw into gold," he said, looking into her eyes, "I will marry you."

When Daisy called for help, the goblin came through the trap door once more.

"I will help you," he promised, "if you give me something precious."

"But I have nothing left!" sobbed poor Daisy.

"Then when you are queen you must give me your first child," he said firmly.

Daisy was shocked.

"I can't give you my child!" she cried.

"Then I won't help you," replied the goblin, "and the king will know you tricked him."

Daisy did not want the king to be angry with her.

"I may never have a child," she thought to herself, "or the goblin may forget my promise."
She turned to the goblin and said, "Very well. I promise I will give you my first child."
So once more, the goblin spun the straw into gold.

In the morning, the king was delighted.
"Now I will make you my wife!" he declared.

And so, the king and Daisy were married. Daisy became queen and in time she forgot about the goblin and her promise. Eventually, Queen Daisy had a baby boy.

The king and queen loved their little prince more than all the gold in the world.

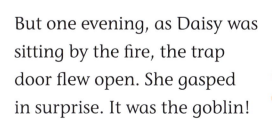

But one evening, as Daisy was sitting by the fire, the trap door flew open. She gasped in surprise. It was the goblin!

"I am here to collect the child you promised me," he said. Daisy burst into tears. "No!" she cried. "I will give you anything, but not my son."

"Then let's play a game," the goblin said with a wicked smile. "I'll give you three days to guess my name. If you guess right, you may keep the child. If not, then you must keep your promise."

Daisy began to guess.

"Hansel?" she asked.

"No," said the goblin.

"Jack?"

"No," said the goblin.

Daisy tried once more.

"Humpty?"

"No." The goblin shook his head.

"I'll come back tomorrow."

The next day, Daisy began to guess again.
"Georgie Porgie?"
"Yankee Doodle?"
"Peter Piper?"

"No, no, no," said the goblin. "Tomorrow is your last day," he warned, and he left through the trap door.

But this time, clever Daisy followed him.
She crept behind the goblin down a dark tunnel,
under the palace, through a gate and into the woods.

There she saw the goblin, dancing by
his camp fire and singing:
"The queen will lose my game!
It really is a shame!
She's in a mess;
She'll never guess:
Rumpelstiltskin is my name!"
"Aha!" whispered Daisy.

The next day, Daisy was ready for the goblin. "What's my name?" he said, moving towards the baby. "You can't guess, can you?"
"Hmm," said Daisy. "Is your name, perhaps, Rumpelstiltskin?"

The goblin was furious. "How did you know?" he shouted, as he stamped his foot on the floor.

He was so angry, and he stamped so hard, that he bounced off the floor and out of the window, never to be seen again.

The queen cuddled her baby. "I'm so glad you're safe," she said.

The king and the queen and their little prince lived happily ever after.

Once upon a time ...

Ideas for reading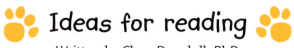

Written by Clare Dowdall, PhD
Lecturer and Primary Literacy Consultant

Learning objectives: Read accurately words of two or more syllables that contain taught graphemes; discuss the sequence of events in books and how items of information are related; become increasingly familiar with and retell a wider range of stories, fairy stories and traditional tales; participate in discussions, presentations, performances and debates; consider and evaluate different viewpoints, attending to and building on the contributions of others

Curriculum links: Music

Interest words: announced, boasted, sobbed, promised, demanded, agreed, cried, declared, warned, whispered, shouted

Word count: 800

Resources: pens and paper for storyboard

Getting started

This book can be read over two or more reading sessions.

- Ask children to recount what they know already about the story and character of Rumplestiltskin.
- Look at the front cover together. Say the name *Rum-ple-stilt-skin,* and count the syllables. Ask children to count the syllables in their name. Discuss how breaking the long word into syllables helps us to read each chunk.
- Turn to the blurb. Read it to the children and ask them to suggest how Daisy will defeat Rumplestiltskin.

Reading and responding

- Ask for a volunteer to read pp 2–3 to the group. Discuss what the simile 'as fair as flowers' means, and what it tells the reader about Daisy.